"No balls inside!" says Mummy.

But Winnie brings her balls inside.

She hides a ball under the rug.

She hides a ball in her bowl.

She hides a ball in Annie's shoe.

Annie finds the balls.

"No balls inside!" says Annie.

But Winnie has one more ball.